GOD IS BIGGER THAN THE BOOGIE MAN

and OTHER BEDTIME STORIES

GOD IS BIGGER
THAN THE BOOGIE MAN
and Other Bedtime Stories

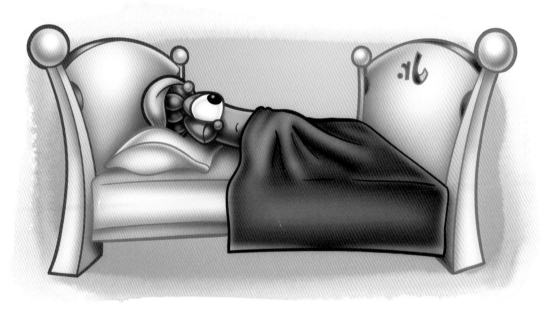

Written by Cindy Kenney
Illustrated by Greg Hardin and Robert Vann

Zonderkidz

www.bigidea.com

Zonder**kidz**™
The children's group of Zondervan
www.zonderkidz.com

God is Bigger Than the Boogie Man and Other Bedtime Stories
Copyright © 2002 by Big Idea Productions, Inc.

Requests for information should be addressed to:
Zonderkidz, Grand Rapids, Michigan 49530

All Scripture quotations, unless otherwise indicated, are taken from the HOLY BIBLE,
NEW INTERNATIONAL READER'S VERSION ®. Copyright © 1995, 1996, 1998 by International
Bible Society. Used by permission of Zondervan. All Rights Reserved.

ISBN: 0-310-70465-0

Library of Congress Cataloging-in-Publication Data

Kenney, Cindy, 1959-
      God is bigger than the boogie man and other bedtime stories / written by Cindy Kenney
   ; illustrated by Greg Hardin and Robert Vann.
         p. cm.
      "Based on the video series, VeggieTales, created by Phil Vischer and Mike Nawrocki."
      Summary: A collection of stories that teach lessons in how to live a good life.
      ISBN 0-310-70465-0
      1. Children's stories, American. [1. Conduct of life—Fiction. 2. Christian life—Fiction.
   3. Short stories.] I. Hardin, Greg, ill. II. Vann, Robert, ill. III. Title.

   PZ7.K3933 Go 2002

                                                                    2002071397

Written by: Cindy Kenney
Editor: Cindy Kenney and Gwen Ellis
Cover and Interior Illustrations: Greg Hardin and Robert Vann
Cover Design and Art Direction: Karen Poth, and Jody Langley
Interior Design: Karen Poth

Printed in United States
02 03 04 05/PC/5 4 3 2 1

Based on the video series: VeggieTales
Created by Phil Vischer and Mike Nawrocki

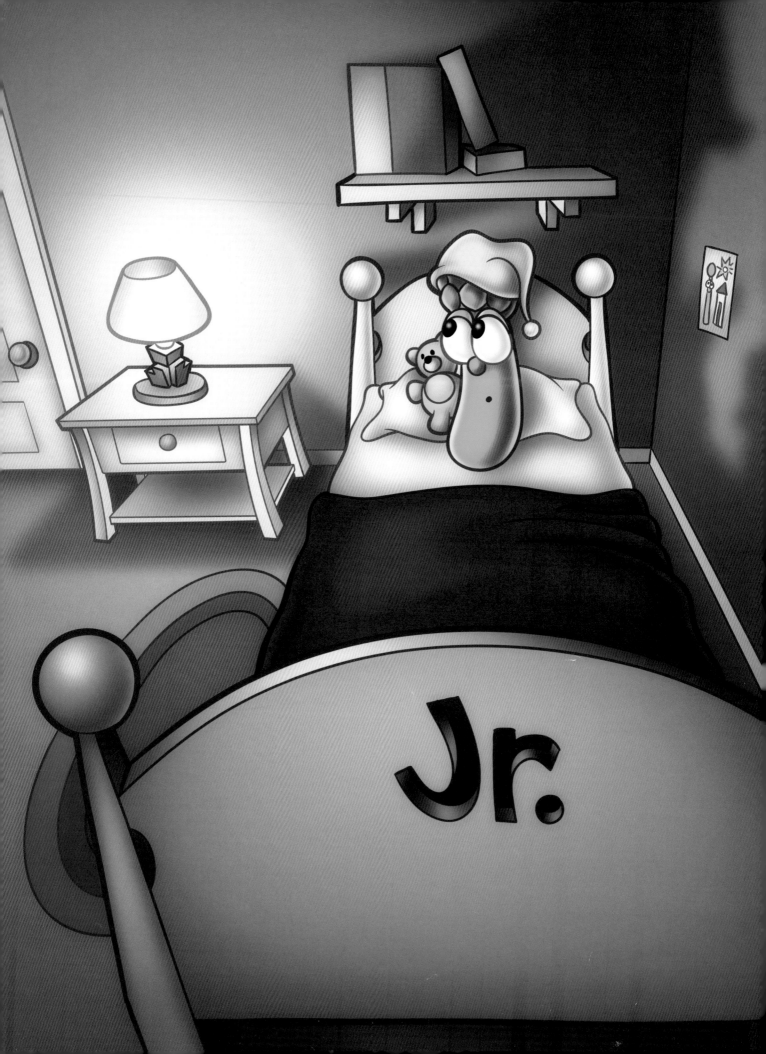

Where is God When i'm scared?

Junior hopped into bed. He was waiting for his dad to come and tuck him in. He was feeling kind of scared and he knew why. He shouldn't have watched another scary television show!

It was only last week that he'd watched a show with FrankenCelery in it. That show was much scarier than he thought it would be when he started watching it! That night, right after he crawled into bed, the most amazing thing happened. He had a visit from Bob the Tomato and Larry the Cucumber!

Bob and Larry sang him a song that really helped him get rid of the willies! How did that song go? Junior tried to remember.

You were lying in your bed
You were feeling kind of sleepy
But you couldn't close your eyes
Because the room was getting...creepy!
Were those eyeballs in the closet?
Was Godzilla in the hall?
There was something big and hairy
Casting shadows on the wall...
Now your heart is beating like a drum,
Your skin is getting clammy.
There's a hundred tiny monsters
Jumping right into your jammies...

Junior was feeling just like that song said right now! He took a big swallow and tried to remember the rest of the words. What were they? Oh yeah, he remembered:

Because God is bigger than the boogie man!
He's bigger than Godzilla,
Or the monsters on TV!
Oh, God is bigger than the boogie man!
And he's watchin' out for you and me!

YES! That was it! God is the biggest! As Junior thought about all this, his fears began to fade away. He sure was glad to know God would always be there to take care of him.

Then Junior looked out his window and saw all the stars in the sky. He remembered how Larry explained that God made all those stars out of nothing! Then Bob told him God also made the sun, the moon and even the whole earth! Junior was quite impressed by all this. After all, even the Slime Monster couldn't come close to doing anything like that!

After a big sigh, Junior settled down under his covers and thought about all the things that God made in the world. Then he remembered that everything God makes is very special to him! He remembered that God made all the little kids and he loves them very much. That was a good thing to remember, especially when he was feeling afraid.

Just then, Junior's Dad peeked in. "Junior, are you ready for bed?"

"I sure am!" Junior answered. "Come on in." Junior and his dad said their prayers together. Then Junior said an extra special thank you to God for taking such good care of everything he created.

"I'm really glad you remembered to thank God for that, Junior," his dad told him as he kissed him on the forehead.

"I don't have to be afraid of stuff because God is on my team!" Junior said.

Then Junior began to sing his own song for his dad.

So when I'm lying in my bed,
And the furniture starts creeping,
I just laugh and say, "Hey, cut that out!"
And get back to my sleeping!
'Cause I know that God's the biggest
And He's watching all the while.
So when I get scared, I think of him,
And close my eyes and smile!
'Cause God is bigger than the boogie man!
He's bigger than Godzilla,
Or the monsters on TV!
Oh, God is bigger than the boogie man!
And He's watchin' out for you and me!

"I like that song, Junior," his dad told him. "What made you want to sing it tonight?"

"Well, I watched a pretty scary television show again tonight," Junior admitted.

"Oh, I thought we agreed to be a little more careful about what we watch on television," his dad reminded him.

"You're right. I guess I forgot. It's just that sometimes when the show starts, it looks like it will be really good. But then, all of a sudden, it starts getting really scary!" Junior said as his eyes grew wide.

"I'll tell you what, Junior. How about if you come and talk to your mom and me the next time you're not sure what a show is going to be about? Then we can help you make a decision about what to watch. Or maybe we can just watch it with you!"

"That sounds like a great idea, Dad! Thanks!"

"You're welcome, Junior. Now get some sleep. I love you, Little Mister."

"I love you too, Big Mister!" Junior said with a yawn.

Then his dad left the room and closed the door. Junior looked around once more at the big, dark shadows on the wall. Then he closed his eyes and remembered that God is bigger than the boogie man, and he's watchin' out for you and me!

"So do not be afraid. I am with you."
—Isaiah 41:10

Madame Blueberry Learns to Be Thankful

It was the end of a very long day. The sun was setting, and streaks of pink, purple, and red were painted through the sky above Madame Blueberry's tree house.

Inside, her butlers, Bob the Tomato and Larry the Cucumber, were busy preparing tea.

"Here's your tea," Bob announced to Madame Blueberry who was sitting on her sofa looking very tired. "You're not feeling blue again, are you?"

Madame Blueberry was usually a very blue berry. She would often break into a song of complaining, wishing for so many things she did not have! Until one day, when she learned a valuable lesson about being thankful.

Madame Blueberry looked up at her loyal butlers, and once again, broke into a song.

I lost all I had, yes, so many things
My toaster, my TV, my alarm clock that sings.
My washer, my dryer, my dishes that were chipped
My curlers, my makeup, and my jammies that were ripped.

There once was a time when I felt oh so blue
I'd reach for my hanky, and you know what I'd do!

I'd sing...I'm so blue-hoo-hoo, blue-hoo-hoo, blue-hoo-hoo hoo!
I'm so blue I don't know what to do!

But I learned a lesson, my friends have been kind
I'm thankful that God has helped me to find
That he has provided for all that I need
He taught me a lesson and planted a seed.

I won't be complaining or crying a lot
I'm quite thankful now that I know what I've got
I have friends that care, and God loves me too,
I'm so thankful, and no longer blue!

"But putting your house back together sure is hard work!" Larry reminded Madame Blueberry when her song was done.

"It certainly is," agreed Bob. "We need to be thankful we have lots of friends to help us!"

"Wouldn't it be great if we had one of those super-sized forklifts that would help us carry everything we need right up to the house?" Larry suggested.

"Well, sure, Larry, but…" Bob tried to say.

"And wouldn't it be cool if we had a helicopter that could drop stuff in through the roof?" Larry added.

"Well, yes, but…" Bob tried again.

"And wouldn't it be even cooler if we had a conveyor belt that went right from the Stuff Mart all the way up to the door so that we could…"

"Larry!" "Yeah, Bob?"

"You're forgetting something."

"I am?" Larry asked. He thought for a minute. "Are you referring to one of those jumbo trucks with the doohickey in back that lets you unload stuff with one push of a lever?"

"Do you mean a forklift doohickey?" asked Bob. "Oh, yeah," Larry remembered.

"No! I'm talking about a happy heart," Bob explained.

"Great idea! We should get one of those, too!" Larry agreed.

"Larry, a happy heart doesn't come from a store. A happy heart is a thankful heart," Madame Blueberry reminded her friend. "I may be tired after trying to put my house back together again, but I know that God will watch over me. I have everything I need that's truly important. I have good friends to help take care of me, like you and Bob."

"And a new day to look forward to after we get some rest," Bob added.

"I guess you're right," Larry conceded. "I suppose that means the forklift is out, huh?" he asked with a wink.

Madame Blueberry and Bob just looked at him as they began to sing.

I thank God for this day
For the sun in the sky,
For my mom and my dad,
For my reasons not to cry.
For my friends that all care
For his love that's everywhere
That's why I say thanks every day!

Because a thankful heart is a happy heart!
I'm glad for what I have.
That's an easy way to start!
For the love that he shares,
'Cuz He listens to my prayers.
That's why I say thanks every day!

"Give thanks to the Lord, for he is good. His faithful love continues forever."
—Psalm 136:1

King George and His Duckies

King George was anxious to take his last bath of the day. It had been such a busy day! First, he had learned a lesson about selfishness. Then, he had tried to help Thomas by returning his duck. He felt good about that decision! In fact, he was thinking of giving almost all of his duckies to boys and girls in the kingdom who didn't have any duckies at all!

"Louis!" King George called to his faithful servant and friend.

"Yes, King George, what is it?" Louis answered from the other side of the king's bathroom door.

"I have an idea!" King George opened the door and hurried over to his closet full of ducks.

"You see all these duckies?" King George asked, as he pulled the closet doors open.

"Of course, I do!" Louis replied, as several duckies came tumbling out.

"I think we should donate these duckies to all the boys and girls in the kingdom who don't have any duckies at all! After all, if I get in the bathtub with all these duckies, pretty soon there won't be room for me!" The king took a ducky out of the closet and gave it squeeze.

"That's a wonderful idea, Your Highness!"

"Sing with me Lewis," King George commanded.

Some kings love horses...
And some kings love cattle.
Some kings love leading their
troops into battle!
But me, I'm not like that...
I find that stuff—yucky!
I'd much rather share some things
like my ducky!

"After all, Louis, I love my ducks!" the king added. " But I also love all the people that God created in my kingdom!"

"That's very true, Your Highness!" Louis was so pleased by the king's change of heart.

"Perhaps we can ask Thomas to help us with this mission, Louis!" the king proclaimed.

"That's a fine idea, Sir. I'll call him tomorrow."

"But right now, I must take my bath, Louis!" the king reminded him.

After King George's bath was ready, he got into the soapy water with his favorite ducky. He gave his ducky a squeeze and began making plans to share his other duckies with all the boys and girls of the kingdom.

"Prepare the duckies, Louis!" King George called out. "We'll go to Thomas' house first thing in the morning and make our deliveries."

"Yes, Sir!" Louis answered with a smile. But before he left to get the duckies ready, he listened as King George sang this song.

> Oh, bein' selfish... Doesn't pay.
> I tried it...Just the other day.
> I wanted to be happy — I thought it was the way,
> But it weren't!

Louis frowned as he listened to the king. He still hadn't gotten the grammar in that song quite right. "I think you mean 'wasn't'! It 'wasn't' the way!" he called out to the king.

Well, now I know... Just what to do!

Before I think about me, I'd better think about you!
So send the message out... To every boy and girl:
There's no better way to make a really yucky world...
Than being selfish! It doesn't pay!
I tried it... Just the other day.
I wanted to be happy—I thought it was the way,
But it weren't, weren't... weren't... weren't!

"Wasn't!" Louis called back. " It wasn't the way."

But King George continued to sing his song...

"Weren't, weren't...weren't...weren't.
No, it weren't!"

Louis sighed. Grammar isn't always everything. At least the king had learned not to be selfish. That seemed to be a whole lot more important.

Louis went to the closet to prepare the duckies to be given away to the boys and girls of the kingdom. And it wasn't long before he began humming...

"I wanted to be happy — I thought it was the way,
But it weren't, weren't... weren't... weren't

No, it weren't...weren't...weren't... weren't
No, it weren't!"

"Don't do anything only to get ahead
Don't do it because you are proud
Instead, be free of pride.
Think of others as better than yourselves.
None of you should look out just for your own good.
You should also look out for the good of others."

—Philippians 2:3-4

Junior Learns How Important it is to Tell the Truth

Time to get ready for bed, Junior," his mom told him right after they got home from their big adventure.

What a day it had been! Junior sure was glad that the truth had come out about breaking his dad's Art Bigotti collector's plate. Junior had told a fib, and it was a scary experience! That fib just kept growing and growing and growing! It was amazing how fast something like that could get out of control.

Junior went upstairs to get ready for bed. In the hallway he passed some toys, and remembered that his mom had asked him to put them away earlier in the day. Junior had promised he would. But there they were!

"Wow! Not doing what I promised is another way to start a fib," he whispered to himself. So he scooped up the toys and took them to his room for safe-keeping.

Junior put on his jammies and went to brush his teeth. Uh oh! He had forgotten to brush his teeth today! Every morning, his mom asked him if his teeth were clean. Had he fibbed about that, too? Junior looked at his toothbrush. "I better brush them twice!" he said, and he promised himself he wouldn't forget again in the morning.

After his teeth were shiny clean, he straightened up his room. That's when he saw a note reminding him to call Percy Pea. They had made a deal to go to the park together. Percy had ridden bikes with Junior the day before, and in return they were supposed to go to the park today. With all the trouble Junior had gotten himself into by telling a fib, he had forgotten all about it! Did not going to the park mean he had told another fib to Percy?!?

Just then Junior's dad came in the room. He saw the startled look on Junior's face and said, "What's wrong?"

Junior explained his dilemma. "Everywhere I look, I see something that could be a fib! I don't want to be a fibber," Junior assured his father. "I told Percy I'd go to the park with him today, and I didn't go."

"I think Percy will understand about going to the park," his dad explained. "Especially if you go there with him tomorrow."

"Fibs are pretty scary things, Dad," Junior said. "They can pop up practically anywhere!"

"If you just remember to tell the truth, things will turn out okay," his dad told him.

"You can say that again," Junior agreed with a smile.

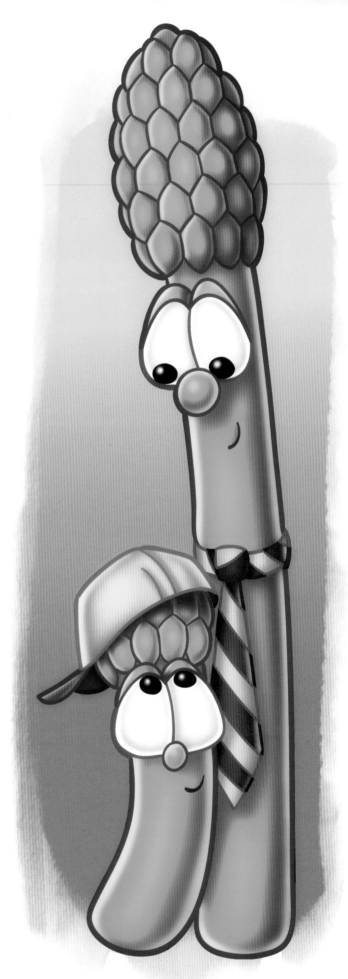

Junior snuggled into bed. Then he and his dad prayed and thanked God for the day, for their friends, and for each other. They also thanked God for teaching them how important it is to tell the truth.

"Goodnight, Dad!"

"Goodnight, Junior," his dad said as he turned the light off. "And remember…God thinks you're special!"

"And he loves you very much!" added Junior before he fell fast asleep.

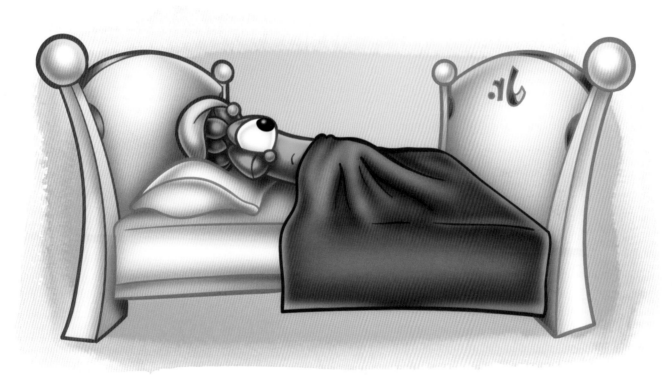

"But those who live by the truth come into the light.
They do this so that it will be easy to see that what
they have done is with God's help."
— John 3:21

Stand Up for What You Believe!

Rack, Shack, and Benny were on their way home after a long day at work. What a day it had been! They'd spent part of the day in a fiery furnace. Then they taught Mr. Nezzer a really big lesson about how important it is to stand up for what you believe. They sure were glad that Mr. Nezzer had learned his lesson well! And they were really glad that they trusted God and that he saved them.

"Hi, guys!" Laura Carrot called out to Rack, Shack, and Benny as she tried to catch up with them. "Nice job at the factory today!"

"Thanks!" Rack answered. "We sure appreciated all your help, too!"

Laura was really pleased that she had helped her friends stand up to Mr. Nezzer. "I'm glad I could help today," she told them. "I think you taught everybody a lesson!"

"Well, it all started by remembering what our parents taught us," Shack explained. "They always said that too much candy isn't good for us. I just reminded Rack and Benny that we shouldn't eat too much chocolate."

So even though we wanted to eat lots of chocolate, we didn't," Rack added.

Then Rack, Shack, and Benny began to sing the song that their parents sang to them.

Think of me every day. Hold tight to what I say,
And I'll be close to you even from far away.
Know that wherever you are, it is never too far.
If you think of me, I'll be with you.

"My mom taught me lots of good things, too! But sometimes it's hard to remember those things. Especially when somebody wants you to do something wrong," Laura said.

Everyone nodded in agreement.
"Just remember how much your mom and dad love you, Laura. That will help you hold onto what they say!" Benny explained.

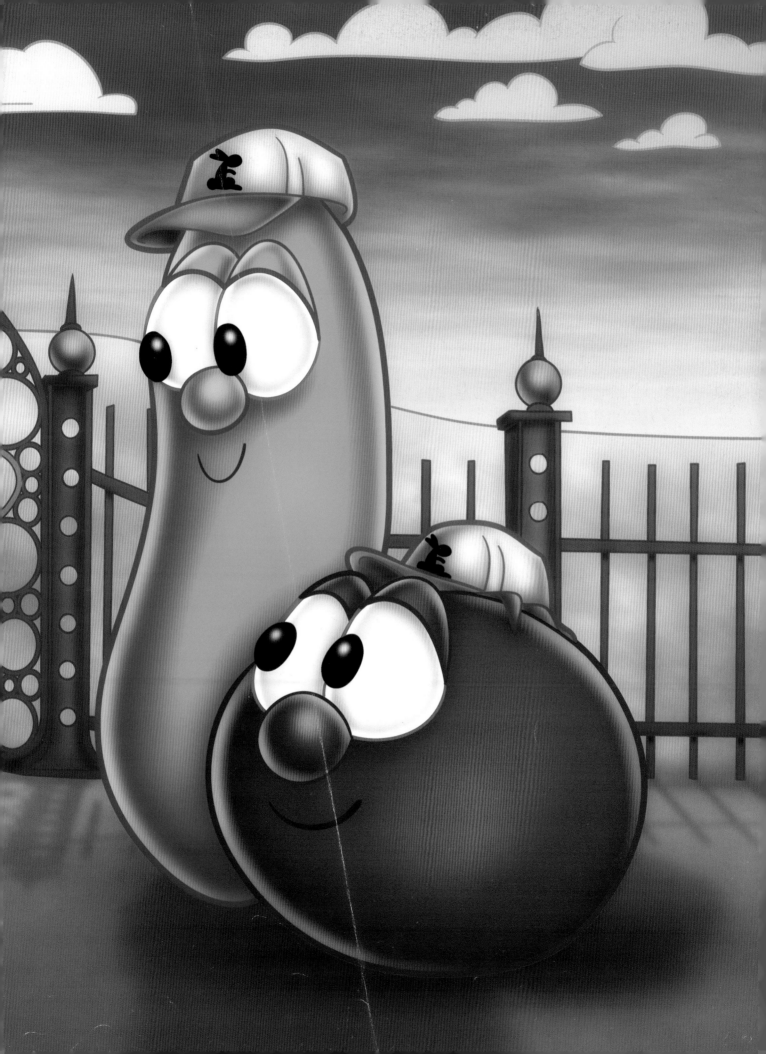

"Your parents try to teach you what God wants you to do. And God's way is always the right way!" Rack added.

"Okay, thinking about that makes it a little easier, then!" Laura agreed.

"Way to go, Laura!" Shack told her. Then he looked at Benny. His friend was frowning.

"What's wrong Benny? Why the big frown?

"Oh, it's just that I like to do so many things!" he said with visions of all sorts of things dancing in his eyes.

"Well, that's okay, Benny," Rack told him.

"But what if I want to do those things more than the things that I'm supposed to do? Like eating chocolate bunnies instead of my salad? Or playing outside instead of doing my homework? Or watching television instead of picking up all my toys?"

"Doing what you want isn't bad, as long as you also remember to do what your mom and dad want you to do first," Shack explained.

"If you remember to follow God's way and do what's right, there will still plenty of time to do the things you like to do!" Rack added.

"You might even discover how good it feels to do what God wants!" Laura added. "Just like today. Didn't it feel great to teach Mr. Nezzer about standing up for what you believe? He learned how important it is to listen to God."

"Ya, that did feel pretty good!" Benny agreed.

"And when you pick up your toys, you're helping your mom and dad. They do so many nice things for you, that it sure feels good to do something nice for them in return!" Shack pointed out.

"Hey! I never thought about that!" Benny said.

"And going to school...well, that's pretty good too. At least we learn a lot of cool stuff there!" Laura told him.

Rack, Shack, Benny, and their friend Laura agreed that following God's way is always the best way...even when something else sounds better at the moment. So they began to sing!

The bunny. The bunny.
The bunny sure is yummy!
But when I eat too much,
it makes my tummy funny.
I wanna do a lot of things,
but first, I'll stop to see
If what I do is right
so that God is pleased with me.
I need to remember that God cares a lot.
He is my friend, and the best one I've got!

Rack, Shack, and Benny sang that song all the way home. It was a good lesson to remember, and they were glad they had the chance to tell others about it!

"Finally, my brothers and sisters,
always think about what is true.
Think about what is noble, right and pure.
Think about what is lovely and worthy of respect.
If anything is excellent or worthy of praise,
think about those kinds of things.
Do what you have learned or received or heard from me.
Follow my example.
The God who gives peace will be with you."
—Philippians 4:8-9

Lyle and The Kindly Vikings

Mabel was rushing around getting some things ready for Lyle and the others to take to the monastery on their next trip out there. As she did, she noticed something sitting on the table beside her bed. It had a small note attached to it.

"Dear Mabel, I thought I would share a potholder with you," she read out loud. The note was signed from Lyle. Mabel held the pretty little potholder up and admired Lyle's work.

"This is lovely!" she cried. Then she hurried out to the next the room to show the others.

Ottar, Sven, Harold, Eric, and Olaf rushed over to see what Mabel was waving in the air. "Ooo!" and "Ahhh!" they said, as they looked at the designs woven into the little potholder.

"Lyle made that?" Ottar asked.

"Yes! He said he wanted to share with me! Wasn't that thoughtful?" she asked. Everyone nodded and broke into a song.

We used—to care, about—our share
Of gold—so rare, and big TVs!
But when—we share, we get—our share, of friends!
So what's—the use? A golden goose, is no—excuse, for being mean!
When—we share, we get—our share, of friends!

Lyle came in at the end of the song, delighted to hear his friends singing about sharing.

"Lyle! Where have you been?" asked Sven.

"I stayed to help my friends clean up after our celebration at the monastery," he said. "We can share our time with others, too! And we can do that by lending a helping hand!"

Everyone looked around at one another. Did they all agree? Harold and Erik looked a little confused. Ottar and Sven frowned. Just then Mr. Lunt walked in.

"What's going on?" Mr. Lunt asked

"Lyle says we should share more than just our stuff!"Sven told him.

"Ya. He says we should also share our time with others!" Erik added.

Everyone began talking at once. What did this mean? The Vikings were a bit concerned. It was one thing to stop pillaging and start sharing their things, but now Lyle wanted them to share their time, too!

"Hey, everybody!" Lyle called out, hoping to get them to settle down for a moment. "Remember the good feeling you got when the monks pulled you out of that stormy sea?"

They all remembered and agreed that was a good feeling.

"And remember that good feeling you got when we decided sharing our things was the right thing to do?" Lyle asked them.

Once again, every-one agreed that sharing was good.

"What's the point you're trying to make, Lyle?" Olaf asked.

"Well, there are lots of ways we can share with others. It doesn't always have to be sharing our toys or potholders. It can also mean taking time to help someone clean up a mess. Or we can help take care of someone who is sick!"

"I don't feel sick," Sven told him.

"What I'm trying to say," Lyle continued, "is that we can all help each other in lots of different ways! It's just another way to share. And when we share…"

"We get our share of friends!" Ottar finished for him. "Right!"

There was a mumbling among the Vikings as they considered this possibility.

"So I could bake something to cheer up someone who is feeling down!" Mabel suggested.

"Or read a story to somebody who isn't very good at reading," offered Sven.

"Now you're getting it!" Lyle said happily.

Within moments everyone was sharing ideas! And soon, everyone began to sing.

We used—to care, about—our share
Of time—so rare, we did not share!
But when—we care, our time—we share
with friends!

So why—not make, some time—and take,
for goodness sake
To help a friend!
Cuz when—we care, our time—we share
with friends!

"And do not forget to do good and to share with others."
—Hebrews 13:16a

The Grapes...
of Nice?

We are the grapes...of math!
We still won't take a bath!
But we'll be nice to men or mice
We meet along our path!

The grapes sang loudly as they bounced along through the countryside on their way home.

"Pa! He's teasin' me about knowin' my math so good!" Rosey complained.

"That's cuz' she thinks she's better 'n me!" Tom whined.

"Now, Rose, we're all real proud that you know your math so good," Pa began.

"Told ya so, you olive-eyed, squished-prune, pizza head!" Rosey gloated.

"Pa!" Tom whined again.

"But that's no reason to think anybody is more special than anybody else. After all, God made everybody special," Pa explained.

"Told you so, you butter-bud, banana-brain!" Tom glared back. "Rose! Tom! Didn't ya learn nothin' today?" Pa asked a bit sternly.

"Well...," Rosey thought. "I reckon so."

"Tell us what ya learned then," encouraged Ma.

"Oh, okay. I learned we're supposed to fergive others.

And he learned that seventy times seven is four hundred and ninety!" Rosey giggled, as she nodded toward her brother.

"Ma! She's startin' all over again!"

"Didn't ya learn anythin' about bein' nice?" Pa asked them.

"I reckon' so," Tom admitted.

"Bein' nice to others means bein' nice to yer brother and sister, too," Ma pointed out.

"I know that!"

Rosey said with a smile. "But it sure ain't any fun!"

Rosey and Tom laughed as the little car hit a big bump in the road, causing everyone to fly momentarily into the air and come down with a thud. The car rolled to a halt.

"That bump was a doozy!" Pa grumbled as he tried to restart the car.

"Everybody okay?" Ma asked, as she looked around.

The kids looked a bit dazed, but appeared to be fine. Tom peeked out from between two seats, and Rosey scrambled back to her seat from the rear of the car.

"Sure, Ma!" Rosey called as she got comfortable again.

"What did ya push me down here fer?" Tom asked his sister.

"I was tryin' to keep ya from fallin' out of the car ya big ole' bazooka ears!" Rosey scowled.

"Who are you callin' a big ole....You what?" Tom asked suddenly. Had he heard his sister right? "Were you really tryin' to do somethin' nice fer me?"

"That was a real nice thing that yer sister did fer ya, back there... whatever it was exactly...that she did there," Pa interrupted.

Rosey smiled. Then Ma smiled. Then Pa and Tom smiled, too. Rosey and Tom even said they'd try to stop calling each other names. But we'll have to wait for the next story to see if that really happened.

Once upon a time, they were the Grapes of Wrath. Then Rosey showed everyone how good she was with numbers, and they considered calling themselves the Grapes of Math.

But then they learned a lesson about forgiveness…and about being nice.

God wants us to show forgiveness to others. He wants us to love one another and treat others the way we want to be treated. And God wants us to start by doing right in our very own families!

"The Lord has shown you what is good.
He has told you what he requires of you.
You must treat people fairly. You must love others faithfully.
And you must be very careful to live
the way your God wants you to."
—Micah 6:8

Love Your Neighbor

The boy with the pot from Jibberty Lot
Returned the next day, although it was hot.
He wanted to see the man he'd befriended
To give him his shoe and see how he'd mended.

His cucumber friend said, "You're back with my shoe!"
You've walked all the way to Flibber-o-loo!
I hope that you'll stay and talk for a bit
I want to say 'thanks!' So I hope that you'll sit."

And so the boy sat, and they talked for a spell
About what had happened and gone so well
Since the boy with the pot from Jibberty Lot
Had helped the cucumber out of that spot.

Both Jibberty Lot and Flibber-o-loo
Had learned to be neighbors and love others, too
They now understood how important it was
To be kind to each other and all that it does.

Take, for example, what the mayor now knew
He respected all towns—even Flibber-o-loo.
And the doctor, she, too, had learned quite a lot—
To make time for others, wearing shoes or a pot.
And those Flibbian friends could now be heard singing
A song through their towns with a new message ringing!

We're busy! Busy! Dreadfully busy!
But we learned a lesson of
what we should do!
Busy! Busy! Shockingly busy!
But never too busy for you!

So the boy with the pot from Jibberty Lot,
And his friend with the shoe from Flibber-o-loo,
Talked for a while, quite pleased that they got,
A chance to learn better just what we should do.

When you see a person in trouble or need,
Perhaps you'll remember to do a good deed.
'Cuz God made them special, just like he made you.
We can all love each other like God wants us to.

"Jesus replied, 'Love the Lord your God with all your heart and with all your soul.
Love him with all your mind. This is the first and most important commandment.
And the second is like it. Love your neighbor as yourself.'"
—Matthew 22:37-38